MW00990722

The Legend of
Chris Moose ™
A Christmas Story

Written by Allen Northcutt
&
Illustrated by Christie Morris

www.thelegendofchrismoose.com

The Legend of Chris Moose

Library of Congress Cataloging-in-Publication Data has been applied for.
The Legend of Chris Moose by Allen Northcutt.
ISBN: 978-1-938462-01-6
Editing by Jill Johnson Keeney
Book Design & Illustrations by Christie Morris

Published by Old Stone Press
Louisville, Kentucky 40207
Enhanced Edition, 2012
Printed in the United States by Bookmasters, Inc.
30 Amberwood Parkway, Ashland, OH 44805
September 2012 Job# M9993

Written by Allen Northcutt

"A Special Thanks to my many friends

who helped bring Chris Moose© to life:

Alix, Anne, Bob, Charles, Christie,

Cindy, Courtney, Dan, Deborah, Dee,

Dolores, Donny, Doug, Ella, Ellen,

Eric, Erin, Frances, Georgie, Ginny,

Graham, Hunt, JD, Jeff, Jim, Joel,

John, Jill, Judy, Katherine, Ken, Mary,

Nana, Randy, Robert, Scott, Shelia,

Talmage and Weasy!" ~ Allen

'Twas the day before Christmas,
and the forest was humming.
The animals were busy,
a big party was coming!

The bears had the party
at their home all aglow.
And Ugly the Moose carried
his friends through the snow.

Now, Ugly didn't like his name –
no, he didn't like it one bit.
But when he saw his reflection
he saw how it fit.

Yes, he was ugly,
all shaggy and tattered.
But the animals all loved him,
and that was what mattered.

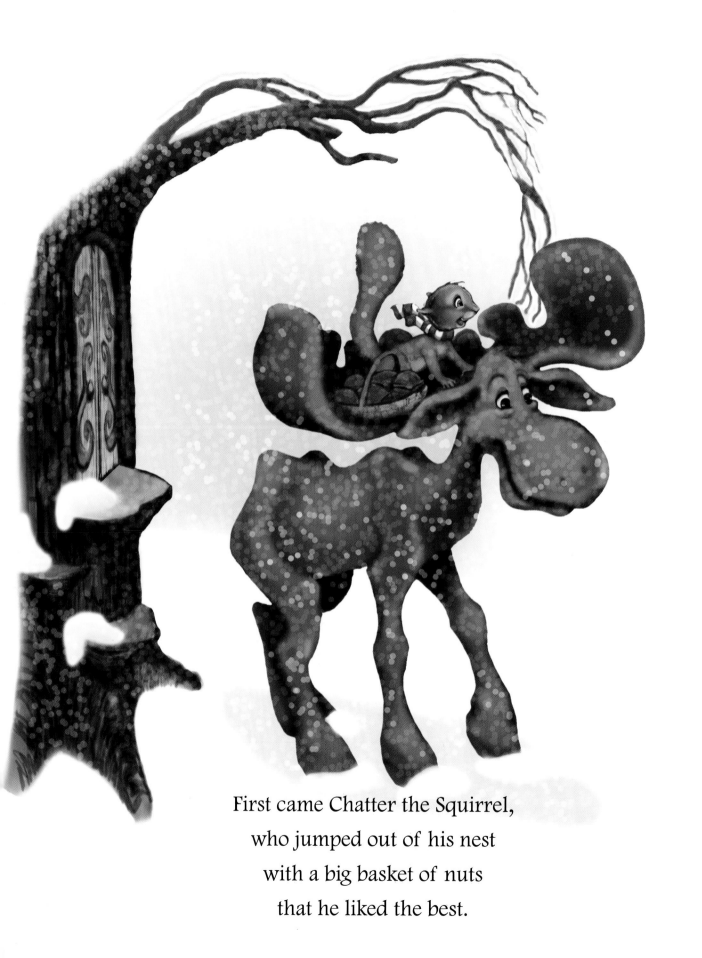

First came Chatter the Squirrel,
who jumped out of his nest
with a big basket of nuts
that he liked the best.

Then they picked up Stinky,
a black and white skunk.
He brought all their stockings,
which he kept in a trunk.

Nosey the Rabbit
brought carrots for snacks,
and a beautiful candle
made of red wax.

Then wearing his mask
came Bandit the Raccoon,
with rings on his tail
and carrying a balloon.

With a big hunk of cheese
came Squeaky the Mouse.
He kept it safe
in the wall of his house.

There was Pokey the Turtle
with a basket of clams,
and lots and lots
of sweet-tasting jams.

Old Smarty the Fox
brought berries to eat,
in a pretty red box –
Oh my! What a treat!

Honker the Goose
had a basket of corn.
When she saw the group coming,
she honked on her horn.

Then Slim the Snake
crawled out on his belly
with a carton of cookies
and a jar full of jelly.

Finally, Hooty the Owl
swooped down from above
and perched on Ugly's antlers
with the friends that he loved.

When they arrived at the Bears' house,
Ugly knocked on the door.
But there was no answer,
so he knocked ten times more.

At last Momma Bear appeared,
very upset.
She and Poppa Bear
had long overslept.

"The house is a mess.
What can we do?"
"Don't worry," said Chatter.
"We'll clean it for you!"

"But how can I help?"
poor Ugly cried.
"I'm too big to fit
all of me inside."

"I want to be part of the group –
to join in the play –
and not be outside, alone
on this Christmas Day."

Then with everyone's help
the house got clean as could be.
But, oh my goodness!
Poppa had slept through getting a tree!

To find a good tree
was a mountain away,
and too far to go
before Christmas Day.

So they piled up their presents
with hearts full of glee.
But something was missing.
"We must have a tree!"

They thought and they thought,
"Oh, what can we do?"
Then Ugly spoke up,
"Will my antlers do?"

"I brought no gift to put on the shelf.
But open that window – I'll give part of myself."

They opened the window as wide as could be,
so Ugly's antlers could serve as their tree.

With popcorn and tinsel
and an angel of gold,

Ugly became
a sight to behold.

But the gift to his friends of himself as the tree
made them rethink his bad old name, Ugly.

They tried lots of names, but all seemed to miss
till Smarty the Fox thought up the name Chris.

"We won't call him 'Ugly.'
Chris Moose is his name.
It sounds so much like 'Christmas,'
it could be the same!"

Then the animals started rockin'
as they danced and they twirled.
And Chris Moose became known as
the Most Beautiful Moose in the World.

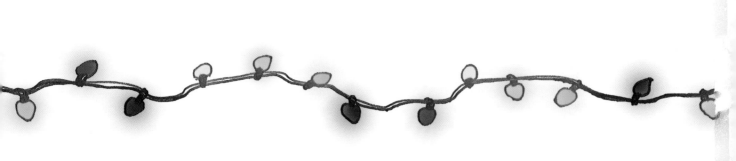